# THE WARRIOR'S ROAD

# SLIVKA
## THE COLD-HEARTED CURSE

*With special thanks to Allan Frewin Jones*
*For Lila, in honour of her own Walk*

www.beastquest.co.uk

ORCHARD BOOKS
338 Euston Road, London NW1 3BH
*Orchard Books Australia*
Level 17/207 Kent St, Sydney, NSW 2000

A Paperback Original
First published in Great Britain in 2013

Beast Quest is a registered trademark of Beast Quest Limited
Series created by Beast Quest Limited, London

Text © Beast Quest Limited 2013
Cover and inside illustrations by Steve Sims © Orchard Books 2013

A CIP catalogue record for this book is available from
the British Library.

ISBN 978 1 40832 404 2

3 5 7 9 10 8 6 4 2

Printed in Great Britain by CPI Group (UK) Ltd, Croydon, CR0 4YY

The paper and board used in this paperback are natural recyclable
products made from wood grown in sustainable forests. The
manufacturing processes conform to the environmental regulations of
the country of origin.

Orchard Books is a division of Hachette Children's Books,
an Hachette UK company

www.hachette.co.uk

# SLIVKA
# THE COLD-HEARTED
# CURSE

## BY ADAM BLADE

ORCHARD

The Warrior's Road

COSHTIN PROVINCE

PYRUS

THE LAST CITY

MARBLE CASTLE

Greetings, whoever reads this.

I am Tanner, Avantia's first Master of the Beasts. I fear I have little time left. My life slips away, and I write these few words as a testament for whoever may come across my remains. I have reached the end of my final journey. But a new warrior's journey is just beginning...

With the death of a Master, a new hero must take on the responsibility of guarding the kingdom of Avantia. Avantia needs a true warrior to wear the Golden Armour. He or she must walk the Warrior's Road – a test of valour and strength. I have succeeded, but it has cost me my life. I only hope those who follow survive.

May fortune be with you,

Tanner

# PROLOGUE

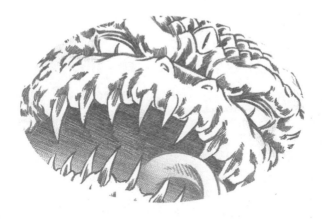

"Curse this foul air!" Colm cried. He coughed, his eyes watering as he pushed through the dense, steamy jungle. Then he turned sharply, peering between the trees. Almost nothing lived so close to the ancient volcano. Only the small yellow frogs that hid in the slimy pools of stagnant water.

Colm moved deeper into the jungle. The only good thing about the foul smell was that no one would follow him this far.

*No one will learn the secret of my poisoned darts*, he thought, smiling grimly. He wiped sweat from his forehead as he parted the ferns, looking for the telltale green shimmer that would mean a pool was nearby.

"Ha! This looks promising," he said. He shouldered his way through hanging vines and came to a narrow stretch of dark green water. The yellow frogs lived in pools like this. Colm was looking for the white clusters of their frogspawn that floated on the scummy surface.

Colm squeezed juices from the spawn to make the most venomous poison in the whole of Coshtin Province. Just a few drops on the tip of one of his needle-sharp darts would be enough to bring down the largest animal.

The scavenger kneeled, taking a long wooden spoon from a satchel at his hip. A glimmer of oozy white goo appeared close to the bank where Colm was crouching. His eyes narrowed as the spawn writhed and bubbled on the water.

"I've never seen that before," he muttered, watching the seething spawn spreading stickily over the water. "Perhaps it's a new kind – even deadlier!"

He was about to dip his spoon into the pool when a shadow fell across the water. *A branch, moving in the wind?* But there was no breeze under the thick canopy of trees. The stinking air was heavy and still, as though the whole jungle was holding its breath.

Colm gave a gasp of fear as he saw a reflection appear in the water. He froze, staring at the mirrored head of a huge lizard. Curved horns jutted forward from the creature's temples and a bony crest rose along its skull. Its jaws gaped to reveal a long flickering tongue between deadly pointed fangs.

But what horrified Colm most were the unblinking eyes. They were slanted and cruel, with greenish-yellow slitted pupils, filled with anger – and there were three of them. The middle eye sat high on the lizard's forehead, between the other two.

Its long forked tongue lashed the air. A disgusting aroma filled Colm's nostrils as the creature let out a menacing hiss.

"Get away from me!" Colm cried. He threw himself forwards into the pool, whimpering with dread as he waded waist deep through the murky green water. He floundered to the far bank and crawled out onto dry land. *Escape!*

But the huge lizard let out a shriek of anger. Even as Colm scrambled to his feet, the lizard leaped across the pool, jaws gaping, claws snatching.

Colm blundered through the close-packed trees. Tendrils and roots grabbed at his feet, branches and hanging vines snagged his body. All the while, he could hear the tearing and crashing of the lizard as it hunted him.

He fought through a veil of hanging tendrils and saw a clear path ahead of him. *Nearly there*, he thought. *If I can just...*

But when he looked back, the lizard had ripped the vines aside. It was scuttling towards him with terrible speed.

*Whack!*

Colm struck a tree trunk at full speed as he ran away. He was flung back. He lay gasping, his whole body hurting, his head spinning.

*Get up, you fool! Run for your life!*

He staggered to his feet, but as he tried to move forwards, something wet and muscular slid around his neck and dragged him back. He felt hot breath on his skin as the lizard gave a delighted hiss.

The creature towered over him, its long tongue tightening around Colm's neck.

Colm choked, clawing at the tongue with both hands. He kicked feebly as the life was squeezed out of him.

There was only one hope left. He released a hand and fumbled in his satchel. His fingers found a dart. He pulled it out, and with his final ounce of strength he stabbed the poisoned dart into the lizard's tongue.

Everything went dark.

# CHAPTER ONE

# FROZEN DANGER

"The Warrior's Road goes that way," Tom told Elenna, his breath coming out in white clouds. He pointed down the snowy slopes of the mountain. "I can see it heading across the plain."

"Towards the frozen lake?" Elenna said, her hands deep in Silver's thick fur. "I'd like to be able to see the Road for myself," she added. "Just once."

Tom knew that Elenna found it

hard to follow him along a road that only he could see. Not that this Quest was any easier for him. His only guide was an old parchment map stained with blood. But at least he'd defeated two Beasts now – Skurik and Targro. *There's some hope*, he thought. *If we can just keep going.*

They'd managed to get warm again after their last Quest by diving into a pool of steaming water, but Tom knew that every second counted if he and Elenna were to survive this cold.

He led his companions down the glowing, rust-red roadway as it wound back and forth across the mountainside. Here, the snow was knee deep and crusted with ice and progress was slow.

At last they stood on the banks of the lake. The ice stretched out in front of them, smooth and featureless.

"Are you sure this is the way?"
Elenna asked, her teeth chattering.

Tom nodded. "We have to trust the
Road," he said. "It hasn't led us astray
so far." The glowing path led straight
ahead across the frozen lake.

Silver whined at their side. Tom guessed that the wolf didn't like the idea of setting out across that great open stretch of ice. He felt the same, but they had no choice. They had to follow the path laid out for them by the Quest, or he would no longer be Master of the Beasts and all of Avantia would be in peril.

They began to cross the lake. A thin, chilling mist wafted in, making it difficult to see more than a few paces ahead.

"This is too dangerous," muttered Elenna as the ice creaked under their feet.

"We can't go back," Tom said grimly. He pointed ahead, his finger tracing the glimmering red line of the road through the white ice. "That's the only way." Suddenly he let out a gasp, his feet faltering. "No!"

"What is it?" asked Elenna, her hands moving to her bow and arrows. "What have you seen?"

"The road has disappeared," said Tom. The red cobblestones were fading from view, one by one.

An ominous crack sounded beneath their feet and the ice shifted a little under them.

"We have to go back," said Elenna.

"No," insisted Tom. "We have to go on. This is the only way to the next stage."

Gritting his teeth, he took a faltering step forward, trying to remember the exact route taken by the vanished road. Elenna and Silver followed reluctantly.

They came to a place where the ice was so thin that they could see the dark water moving beneath it.

A loud snap echoed through the air and Tom felt the ice move under him. He stumbled forwards.

"Jump back!" cried Elenna, holding her hands out. "Quickly!" She and Silver were on a shelf of stable ice, but dark fissures were opening up all around Tom.

"No!" Tom called back. "You have to follow me."

Elenna sprang forward with Silver close at her heels. "You had better be right about this," she said.

Tom began to walk across the swaying ice floe, testing every step before transferring his weight, his arms stretched out for balance. There was a loud snapping sound, like that of a great whip. Tom staggered, losing his footing as a wide crack opened up beneath him. The two halves of the ice floe split apart with a gush of freezing water. Tom clutched frantically at the rearing wall of ice as he slithered down into the water.

He prepared himself for the icy bite of the seething black water – but the water he plunged into was warm and bright and streaked with shafts of golden sunlight.

Holding his breath, he stared around. Elenna and Silver were close by, swimming strongly and cocooned in bubbles.

Then Tom saw a shimmering rust-red shadow beneath him. It was the same colour as the Warrior's Road. He swam towards it, but stopped when he saw the parchment map had come loose from his tunic and was drifting downward, spiralling away from him.

*No! I can't lose the map!*

He twisted in the water, swimming strongly after the map. He snatched for it but the parchment dissolved away to shreds in his hand. Tom hung in the water, too stunned to move.

*Now what? Without the map we're lost! How could I have let this happen?*

He felt a hand grab his collar and he was hauled upwards through the warm water towards bright sunlight.

Elenna towed him to the lake's edge.

Everything was different. A thick, humid jungle stretched out in front of them, roots and tendrils reaching down into the warm water. They'd escaped the cold mountains! The mystical road had led them through another portal.

They clambered out and found Silver on the bank close by. The wolf shook the water out of his fur.

Tom sniffed the foul air, his eyes narrowing at the stink.

"It's like rotten eggs," Elenna said, her hand to her face. "Horrible!"

"But at least we don't have to worry about freezing to death now," said Tom. "And I can see the Road again." He pointed to where the glowing, red road wound off into the thick undergrowth.

"You were right, Tom," said Elenna. "I should have trusted you."

"Don't worry about that now," Tom told her. He just hoped he'd be able to carry on leading them, now that he'd lost the map.

A dull thumping noise sounded from the trees. *The next Beast?*

"Come on, let's investigate," he said, striding ahead. With each footstep, his leather boots squelched in the muddy ground.

Tom led them further into the trees, but suddenly the Road faded again. He paused, puzzled.

"What's wrong?" asked Elenna.

The Road flickered for a moment then vanished.

"It's disappeared again. It keeps coming and going," Tom told her. "Now that I've lost the map, the Road is the only way of knowing we're still on the right track." He looked at Elenna. "If we get lost now, the Quest will truly be over."

# CHAPTER TWO

# POISONED DARTS

Tom waited for the Warrior's Road to reappear.

"This smell reminds me of Stonewin," said Elenna. "Remember? The volcano where Epos lives?"

Tom nodded. How could he forget the hot, barren rock and the rivers of molten flame? But even the volcano had not filled Tom with the same sense of menace as this jungle.

Finally, the Road shimmered into view again, snaking away into the jungle gloom. "Keep close to me," Tom said, forcing his way through the undergrowth. "We mustn't lose one another."

They hadn't gone far when a low, groaning noise sounded close by. Tom halted, lifting his hand. "Did you hear that?" he asked.

It came again. The deep, guttural moan of a man in pain.

Tom moved towards the sound.

"Careful," Elenna warned as she and Silver followed. "We can't trust anyone in this land."

Tom nodded and closed his fingers around his sword hilt. They had been betrayed before on this Quest, and he had no intention of letting his guard down again.

He found a man slumped with his back to a tree. His clothes were in rags and there was a raw red welt around his neck.

"Let us help you," said Tom, reaching down towards the man.

"No!" The man clawed at the air, warding Tom off. " I don't need any help from you."

His half-crazed eyes widened as Elenna and the wolf appeared through the trees. "Keep that thing away!" he shouted frantically. The man pushed himself to his feet, but Tom saw that one of his legs was twisted. As he tried to put his weight on it, he cried out in agony and slumped down again.

"You do need our help," Elenna said. "I think your leg's broken. I'm good at finding healing herbs to relieve pain. Silver, come with me, we need to find some sticks to brace his leg."

Tom sat by the man's side while Elenna and Silver were gone. The man grasped Tom's hand, grimacing in pain.

"What's your name?" Tom asked. "I'm Tom and my friends are Elenna and Silver."

"My name is Colm," said the man, staring wildly into Tom's face. "Did you see the monster?"

Tom's ears pricked up – could Colm be talking about the next Beast?

"It's like a gigantic lizard," muttered the man. "Except that it has three eyes and a murderous tongue."

Elenna and Silver appeared, Elenna carrying several sturdy sticks that were about the length of her arm.

"You need to straighten your leg as much as you can," she told Colm. "This will hurt, but I have to do it if you're ever going to walk properly again."

As Elenna laid the sticks on either side of Colm's injured leg he cried out in pain and clutched fiercely at Tom's arm. Elenna took some lengths of cloth from her bag and gently began to tie the sticks to the leg.

While she worked, Tom told her

what he had learned from Colm.

"Our next foe has awoken," he said. "We have to get Colm back to his home – but then we must find the Beast."

They helped Colm to his feet. With their aid, he began to hobble along.

"This is the way to my village," he told them. "It's a fair distance, but the road through the forest is straight and clear." Tom said nothing, but it worried him that they were moving so far from the Warrior's Road. Would they ever find it again in this huge jungle?

Tom heard swift whizzing sounds coming from ahead of them. *What's going on? Are we being attacked?*

He was reaching for his sword when he felt a sharp sting on his neck and he heard Elenna cry out.

He saw a small slender dart sticking
out of Elenna's neck. He brought his
hand to his own throat and felt a thin
sliver of wood. Wincing, he pulled the
dart out.

A horrible sensation filled Tom, as
though ants were crawling through

his veins. His vision blurred and the forest seemed to twist and writhe around him. His legs felt rubbery, his fingers numb.

"The darts are poisoned!" he gasped. "Elenna – get back." He stumbled and fell, striking the ground hard, a thick fog filling his mind.

As he lay limp and helpless on his back, he heard voices closing in all around him. Elenna was sprawling close by. He saw her try to stand, then collapse.

"Help us," Tom gasped. "We're not your enemies…" He could no longer see the man who'd brought them here.

A dark shape loomed over him. He felt a spear point pressing against his throat.

"You will pay for bringing the Beast

to our village!" said a loud, angry voice. "You will pay with your life!"

# CHAPTER THREE

# THE FIRE RACK

"Wake up! See the death we have planned for you!"

Tom opened his eyes. A dull pain was throbbing through his limbs, and his vision was blurred. He realised with a sickening jolt that he was tied up and hanging at a strange angle. He could feel a fierce, searing heat beating against his face.

The last thing he could remember

was a spear at his throat. *The poisoned dart! I must have passed out.*

Strange shapes loomed around him and now he could feel stinging heat all along the front of his body. Yellow and red flames leaped before his eyes.

"He's awake!" shouted a voice. "Lower them into the fire! They must suffer for bringing the Beast!"

Tom stared around. He was tied to an upright wooden frame that hung on ropes beside a roaring fire. Through the flames he could see Elenna bound to a similar construction.

"Tom!" she called weakly. "We'll get out of this – Silver is still free. He escaped into the jungle."

The large fire was surrounded by people in simple linen clothes and fur skins. Ordinary village folk, but with

angry faces. Beyond the heads of the
people, Tom saw thatched houses and
other wooden barns and workshops.

*This must be Colm's village*, he
thought, wrenching at the rope bonds
with his arms, straining with his legs.

A tall, muscular boy leaped in front

of him, brandishing a broad-bladed spear. Tom guessed the boy was only a few years older than him, but he seemed to be the leader.

"Don't bother trying to escape!" he shouted in Tom's face. "No one has ever escaped the Fire Rack." He gestured with his spear. Tom heard a creaking from the ropes and the wooden frame jerked down, closer to the flames. The heat beat up into his face, making his skin sting and his eyes smart.

"No!" he heard Elenna cry out.

Tom realised that the frames were designed to be lowered slowly into the fire. He and Elenna were going to be burned alive!

"Don't do this," Tom cried. "We didn't bring the Beast here." He stared at the crowd, seeing Colm close by, supported between two of the villagers. "Colm!" he called. "Tell them how we helped you. Tell them we're good people."

But Colm only shook his head. Tom guessed that the pain of his broken leg, and the terror of having faced the Beast had been too much for him.

Tom twisted painfully round to face the boy with the spear. "We've come here to fight the Beast," he said.

The older boy stared into Tom's face. "You want me to believe that a boy like you could fight the great lizard?" he scoffed.

"I come from a kingdom far away," Tom said loudly, looking straight into the boy's eyes. "I may be young, but I am the strongest warrior in Avantia, and the only person strong enough to defeat the Beast. Release me and I will prove it to you."

The boy grabbed Tom's hair
and lifted his face. "You're a great
warrior?" he said. "I laugh at such
nonsense!"

Tom could see the glimmer of pride
in the boy's eyes. Could Tom use this
pride to get the better of him?

"Then prove it's not true," Tom said

loudly enough for everyone to hear. "Fight me. I will show my strength by beating you."

Tom heard murmurs from the crowd. A voice called out. "Fight him, Jenko – kill him with your own hands!"

Tom held his opponent's gaze as Jenko's eyes blazed with anger. "Or are you too scared to face me?" he asked.

Snarling, Jenko shoved Tom hard in the chest, lifting the frame and sending it crashing backwards into the dirt. Tom gasped and winced at the juddering pain of the impact. *But my plan is working!*

Jenko pulled the knots loose from around his body. A few moments later, Tom was able to stand up. He nursed his bruised and grazed wrists, watching Jenko carefully.

"Release my friend as well," Tom demanded, pointing to Elenna.

"If you defeat me, she will be set free," snarled Jenko. "If you lose, you will both be fed to the flames."

"Agreed," said Tom. He looked around and saw that his sword and shield had been dumped a little way from the fire. He made towards them.

Jenko snatched at his arm. "No!" he said. "We do not fight with toys here."

He pulled a long spear from the ground. Someone handed another spear to Tom. He hefted it in his hands, testing the weight and balance of the unfamiliar weapon.

The villagers had formed a wide circle away from the fire and more people were joining them.

"Jenko – the evil dog cannot be found," someone called from among the newcomers. "It may have been killed and eaten by the great lizard."

*Evil dog?* Tom smiled to himself – they meant Silver. Elenna said he had escaped into the jungle.

"You're smiling?" Jenko shouted to Tom. "You think you can beat me?" With a roar of pure rage, he flung himself forwards with Tom's death in his eyes.

# CHAPTER FOUR

# THE DESPERATE DUEL

Tom spread his feet, his knees flexed, his fingers tightening around the shaft of the spear. He shook his head, trying to fight the after-effects of the poisoned dart.

He followed the fierce boy's every move, preparing himself to parry the moment that Jenko came in range.

Yelling wildly, Jenko bore down on

him. Tom bounded aside, bringing
his own spear around to strike a
sharp blow on his attacker's shoulder.
The enraged boy let out a howl
of frustration, stumbling from the
impact and almost falling.

Jenko spun on his heel. His lips were drawn back in a snarl as he rushed at Tom again. Gripping his own spear, Tom fended off the blow and danced aside as Jenko staggered, unbalanced by his own momentum.

The other boy charged a third time, and again Tom ducked the blow and whacked Jenko as he blundered past. He needed to defeat Jenko as quickly as possible, but he didn't want to do the boy any real harm.

Jenko attacked again, twisting quickly, slashing at Tom so he had to spring backwards to avoid having his stomach sliced open. While Tom was still on the back foot, Jenko charged with the spear lifted high above his head, the point aimed at Tom's throat.

There was a roar of approval from the crowd, then a groan as Tom dived and rolled away. The force of Jenko's strike sent his spearhead deep into the ground. Tom swung his spear and brought the butt end down across Jenko's back. He was still determined not to use the point. He wanted to win without drawing blood if he could.

Jenko wrenched his spear from the ground. The two boys faced one another, crouching low. They circled slowly, Tom watching Jenko's every move.

*Will I have to use the blade on him after all?*

The muscular boy was powerful, but he wasn't a seasoned fighter, Tom could already tell that. He relied too much on raw strength and not enough on battle-hardened skills.

"Keep your distance," Elenna called.

"Wear him down."

Jenko lunged at him, but Tom sidestepped again and twisted around, coming up behind Jenko and forcing the shaft of his spear against the boy's throat. Jenko couldn't move. Tom's trap had worked perfectly.

"Yield!" Tom gasped, adding pressure.

But Jenko elbowed him in the ribs and surged free.

Grimacing in pain, Tom backed off. He was vaguely aware of Targro's claw and the curious resin gloves of Skurik falling from inside his tunic. But he had no time to worry about that now.

*How can I win this fight when I feel so weak? It's only a matter of time before he catches me out.*

He heard Elenna shouting. "Use your amber jewel!"

The amber jewel would certainly improve his fighting skills. But was it allowed?

"No!" he called. "I mustn't give the Judge any excuse to accuse me of cheating." No one who had walked the Warrior's Road in the past had had magical tokens to help them. This fight would have to be boy versus boy, spear versus spear.

Tom let Jenko hurtle towards him, his heart beating fast, his limbs shaking. He dropped to one knee, letting the spear droop in his hands.

The crowd roared. Jenko slowed, walking forwards with a smile on his face.

"Tom, no!" he heard Elenna cry. "Get up! You must get up!"

Jenko towered over him, his spear raised in both hands, the point

gleaming in the firelight. Just before
Jenko brought the weapon down,
Tom gripped his spear and swung it at
the boy's legs.

With a yelp of pain, Jenko fell to his
knees. Tom smacked his spear shaft
across Jenko's knuckles, jarring the
spear out of his hand. With another
sweep of the spear, Tom sent Jenko's
weapon skittering across the ground.

He brought the point of his spear to rest against Jenko's chest.

"Now will you yield?" Tom demanded.

Jenko's shoulders drooped and he lowered his head.

Tom knew that this was as close to an admission of defeat as he would get from Jenko. He stood up, and tossed his own spear aside.

Jenko got to his feet, scowling as he turned and walked away. A few others followed him as he passed through the crowd and disappeared into one of the huts.

"Well done, Tom!" cried Elenna.

Tom saw that all eyes were on him now, and none of them were friendly. There was the murmur of angry voices from the crowd.

A spear sailed through the air and

stabbed into the ground a fraction
away from Tom's feet.

*This isn't over yet!*

# CHAPTER FIVE

# THE SHAMAN'S CAULDRON

"Do no harm to the boy!" A loud voice rang out over the growing muttering of the people. "Stand back!"

Tom watched warily as the crowd parted and a tall, elderly man stepped forward. He was dressed in a long garment of many-coloured leather patches and there were feathers and beads hanging in his long, grey hair

and beard. He had a hooked nose
and sunken cheeks, and under his
sweeping eyebrows his eyes were
fierce and dark.

He walked slowly towards Tom,
holding out a tattered leather satchel.
With his other hand he pointed to
the tokens that had fallen from Tom's

tunic – the claw and the gloves.

"You will need to keep your things safe if you are to walk the pathless jungle," the man said in a deep, powerful voice. "Things kept in this pouch can never be lost. Will you take it?"

"I will, thank you," Tom said, stepping forwards and taking the satchel. "But my friend must be set free now," he added, pointing to Elenna, who was still tied to the Fire Rack.

The man gestured to the villagers. Half a dozen of them ran forwards and hauled Elenna back from the heat of the fire and untied her from the wooden frame.

She came over to Tom and the old man, rubbing her wrists but smiling. Her clothes were speckled with ash and soot and her hair was slightly singed from the heat. "Thank you," she said to the man. "Are you the leader of this tribe?"

The man frowned. "I am, you might say, their guide," he replied slowly. "In some things at least. My name is Arfur. Come, you need rest and comfort after your ordeal." He turned and strode away.

Tom and Elenna glanced at one another. They followed the old man through the crowd that parted silently for them.

"We need to find Silver," Elenna said. "I'm worried about him. It's not like him to go missing when we're in danger."

The branches and leaves of the jungle overhung the small shack, giving it a gloomy, eerie look as they walked in through the creaking cane door.

Tom blinked, waiting for his eyes to adjust to the darkness. Although the air reeked of sulphur outside, within the shack a sweetish smell lingered.

"Don't you have any windows?" Elenna asked the man.

"No, child," replied the man, moving around easily in the deep gloom. "These walls are a barrier to the foul breath of Gogmoth. I burn incense to keep the air wholesome."

Tom was about to ask who Gogmoth was, when the old man lit a lamp set on a table.

Tom gazed in amazement at the strange sights that surrounded them. The walls were hung with bundles of bones and multi-coloured feathers. Strings of herbs were suspended from the roof beams and there were shelves of vials and pots. An iron cauldron stood in one corner, giving off wisps of steam.

"You're a shaman," said Tom, understanding now why the people had obeyed the elderly man.

"That's right. I'm the village's wise man," said Arfur with a nod. His eyes flashed. He shuffled to a corner. "Help me," he said. "And you may learn some of my secrets."

Elenna and Tom ran forwards and helped him to carry the smoking cauldron into the middle of the room. He moved around the shack, taking bottles and phials from the shelves and pouring a strange-smelling, seething brew into the old cauldron. Tom looked on warily as he flung feathers and bones and rune-carved stones

into the mixture.

Sparks flew and a plume of thick crimson smoke rose to the ceiling.

Suddenly the smoke whirled away and Tom gasped to see a clear orb, like a bubble, floating on the surface of the liquid in the cauldron.

"Watch," whispered the shaman. Tom and Elenna edged closer and stooped to look into the orb.

Shapes and colours swirled, then a picture became clear to Tom. He saw a boy, not much older than him, walking down a dusty red path that led towards a fiery volcano. There was something familiar about the figure...

"It's Tanner," Tom gasped. "I know this scene from the ancient Chronicles of Avantia."

"The first ever Master of the Beasts?" murmured Elenna.

"Indeed it is he," muttered the shaman. "It is written that once in every generation, a stranger to Coshtin Province will walk the Road that only he can see and face the Beasts."

The image in the orb began to swirl again until it was just a spinning rainbow of colour. Then the orb sank and the seething brew became still.

Tom turned to Arfur. "Is there a Beast in the jungle now?" he asked.

"The Beast is called Slivka," said Arfur. "I must warn you that your Quest is virtually impossible. None have ever defeated Slivka."

"I have never turned from a Quest," Tom said firmly. "Tell me more."

The old man nodded solemnly. "The Beast has not been seen in these parts for eight generations," he said. "But it has returned now to blight our lives. That is why the people are afraid." He stared into Tom's face. "Are you walking the Warrior's Road, boy?"

Tom nodded, swallowing hard. "I am," he said. "I must find this Beast Slivka and defeat it."

The shaman nodded and drew something from the folds of his robes.

"These were made by Colm," he said, dropping a small bundle of darts into Tom's hand. "Their tips contain a deadly poison so be wary of how you

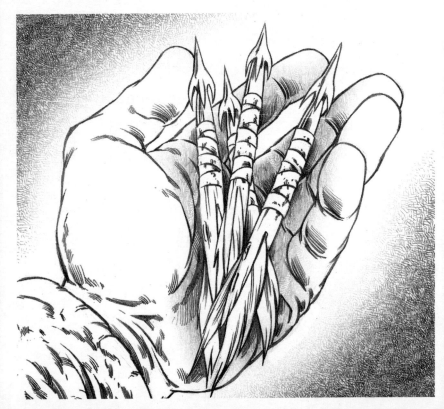

handle them." He strode to the door and threw it open. "Go, now!" he said. "Stay strong, and you may live to follow the path another day."

"Thank you," said Tom as he and Elenna stepped out into the open again. He turned to the shaman. "It's my destiny to walk the Warrior's Road," he said. "And I intend to reach the end!"

# CHAPTER SIX

# GOGMOTH

Some of the villagers had gathered in front of the shaman's shack, watchful but keeping a respectful distance.

Tom's hand moved to his sword hilt.

"They don't look like they mean us harm," said Elenna.

"Good luck, Shaman-friends," called one of the men. "We wish you well."

"Thank you," said Tom as they made their way back through the villagers. He needed to enter the jungle at the same place they had left it if he was to find the Road again.

A few people trailed after them, but as the rotten stink of the air grew worse, they dwindled away.

Tom stepped under the heavy canopy of trees, staring this way and that, moving slowly through the dense undergrowth.

The red path appeared for a moment ahead of them.

"There!" he called, running forwards. Elenna chased him, but in the few moments it took them to get there, the Road had vanished again. "Which way did it go?" Tom muttered. Elenna stood close by, biting her lip

"That way," Tom said at last, certain that he had remembered correctly.

As they headed deeper into the jungle, a long melancholy howl echoed through the trees.

"Silver!" cried Elenna. She cupped her hands around her mouth. "Silver! We're coming!"

They listened but there was no reply from the jungle.

"He's calling to let us know where he is," Elenna said, running wildly through the trees. She shouted again. "Silver!"

Tom raced after her, drawing his sword as they crashed through the jungle. More howls floated on the air.

Elenna paused, turning her head.

"The sound is coming from all around us!" she cried in despair. "Where is he? I must find him, Tom."

"I know," he replied. "But what about the Warrior's Road? We can't lose it completely."

Elenna's hand flew to her mouth. "I've led you off it, haven't I?" she gasped. "Tom, I'm so sorry. What do we do now?"

"See if we can find the Beast," said Tom. "As long as we can still hear Silver, we know he's all right. We'll defeat Slivka, then find Silver. Then we can retrace our steps to the Road."

They pressed on, listening to the occasional howl from Silver. But a new sound rumbled through the jungle – a deep, low grumbling roar.

"The volcano," said Tom. "I think we're getting closer to it – can you smell it? The air stinks far worse now."

Even as the words left his mouth, he heard a rustling sound in the undergrowth close by. His warrior

instincts made him dive aside. Elenna
let out a cry as a powerful tongue
lashed out from deep foliage and
cut into the tree above Tom's head,
leaving a raw white gouge in the
bark.

Tom leaped to his feet with his
sword and shield ready.

But in the few moments before the tongue snapped back and vanished into the dense undergrowth, he saw that it had a raw red wound, as though it had been stabbed with a sharp knife.

*Colm said he used a dart to escape the Beast!*

Elenna put an arrow to her bow, trying to aim for the Beast.

But the jungle was thick and dark and neither Tom nor Elenna could see or hear anything of Slivka.

"Where did it go?" Elenna whispered.

"Hush!" murmured Tom, glancing around. He suddenly glimpsed three glinting eyes among the ferns, slitted and filled with evil intent. "There!" he shouted, lunging forwards.

Tom saw the Beast at last! The huge

lizard towered over him, rising up
onto his hind legs, his body covered
in hard blue scales, his tail lashing

wildly. His forelegs were raised high, and claws reached out like curved swords. Slivka's massive face had three eyes and was crested with bone. Deadly horns jutted forwards like tusks. The jaws gaped wide and red, lined with fearsome fangs.

As Tom flung himself at the Beast, Slivka's tongue lashed out again. It struck the flat of Tom's sword, sending the blade flying back to hit Tom in the face.

Tom dropped dizzily to one knee, half-blinded, his head bursting with pain.

A high-pitched hissing drew closer. Tom could hear the lashing sound of Slivka's tongue. The Beast meant to finish him off, but he was too dazed to do anything more than wave his sword in the air.

Then he heard another sound – a sharp, familiar whizzing. One of Elenna's arrows flashed past him. He heard a shriek of anger and the flickering tongue slid away.

Elenna grasped Tom by the collar and dragged him back through the undergrowth.

"You can't fight the Beast now," she said, pulling him to his feet. "We need to get away so you can recover."

Tom knew she was right – his head was still spinning and he couldn't see clearly yet. They scrambled away, coming suddenly into a wide clearing bordered by a narrow stretch of rock. The surface of the rock was rippled and furrowed in a way that Tom had never seen before.

"It looks like a river that's been turned to stone," said Elenna.

Tom stared across at the dark volcano that filled the sky in front of them.

"It must be cold lava," he said. "From an old eruption."

Thin spirals of smoke rose from the volcano's cone and its sides were streaked with yellow sulphur. Even as he stood marvelling at the mighty volcano, the foul air that was pouring down its sides filled his nostrils and lungs and made him choke. At his side, Elenna held her hand over her mouth, struggling to breathe.

"Gogmoth!" gasped Tom, suddenly realising what Arfur had meant when he'd mentioned "the foul breath of Gogmoth". He'd been talking about the volcano.

A small dark shape came leaping across the river of cold lava.

"Silver!" cried Elenna. "Quickly, Silver! Come to us!"

But the wolf was still only halfway across the lava-bed when a deep rumble sounded from the volcano and Tom felt the ground tremble under his feet.

He stared up at the cone and saw thick grey clouds belching out, rolling up into the sky, lit red from beneath and crowned with white lightning.

Tom's eyes widened in alarm. "The volcano!" he shouted. "Gogmoth is about to erupt!"

# CHAPTER SEVEN

# ERUPTION

There was an ear-splitting roar as geysers of red fire burst from the volcano. Tom was almost knocked from his feet as the ground all around him heaved. Fiery clouds boiled up and spread across the sky, veiling the sun and sending down a rain of hot ashes.

"Silver!" cried Elenna, lunging forwards as the terrified wolf cowered on the old lava river, his belly to the ground and his ears flat along his head.

"No," shouted Tom, holding her back. "It's too dangerous."

She struggled to get loose, but Tom gripped her firmly.

"Call out," Tom insisted. "Make him come to you!"

"Silver!" shouted Elenna over the roaring of the mountain. "Come here, boy!"

The wolf jumped onto a boulder, his eyes reflecting the red light, the hackles stiff along his back.

Tom and Elenna watched as molten rock spewed up in a dazzling orange-red fountain and then came pouring down the mountain's sides. Steam billowed upwards, hissing and spitting. The flow of molten rock had already

reached the stone river and was
sending out fiery red fingers in every
direction. Fortunately they were on
high ground; safe for the moment as
the lava reached the forest and trees
burst into flame all around them.

Tom stared helplessly at the wolf.

*We can't get to Silver in time. He's going to be trapped!*

The lava flowed around his rock, lifting it and carrying it along. Silver cringed away from the heat. Tom could see the rock sinking gradually into the lava.

*The rock is going to be swallowed by the lava. Silver will be killed.*

Elenna ran along the bank of the burning river, but before she or Tom could do anything, Slivka burst out of the jungle, his long tongue flicking, his claws raking the air.

Thinking quickly, Tom snatched up a rock and flung it at the Beast's head.

The rock struck hard. Letting out a screech of rage, Slivka turned, his three dreadful eyes fixing on Tom, his jaws gaping to reveal rows of deadly fangs.

"It's not her you want!" Tom

shouted. "It's me!"

He dashed back into the jungle as Slivka darted towards him, his tail whipping.

Tom jumped up into a tree, scrambling higher as Slivka clawed at the trunk, sending his long tongue lashing up through the branches.

Tom peered down. Slivka was leaping up, trying to grab hold of the lower branches. But he kept falling back, hissing and shrieking.

*He can't climb! That's good, but I need to get down to the ground again to fight him.*

He pushed his way to the top of the tree where the trunk was thin. Taking a firm hold, he swung himself back and forth, then leaped for the next tree.

All around him, the trees were burning. Flames were getting closer all the time. The smell of sulphur was so thick now that Tom could hardly breathe. He carried on jumping from tree to tree, leading the Beast away from his friends, hoping that Elenna would find some way to rescue her beloved wolf.

Tom saw Slivka tracking him as he moved through the treetops. Every now and then the Beast's tongue would lash up through the branches and Tom had to jump aside to avoid being snared. Tom heard a snarl and a slashing, crunching sound as he leaped from one treetop to the next. Slivka was using a new tactic, he realised, tearing the trees down to get at his prey.

Tom leaped again and clung to the high branches of another tree, his limbs aching, his eyes smarting. He felt the tree shudder as Slivka ripped at it with his claws. The tree swayed and Tom heard the trunk cracking under the Beast's raging blows.

All around him the trees were ablaze. He was trapped.

He stared down, seeing Slivka's great claws gouging out chunks and splinters of wood. His heart began to pound, the sweat dripping into his eyes. There was no escape.

Slowly, with loud snaps and cracks, the tree began to topple. Tom clung on grimly as it crashed through the canopy of burning branches and hit the ground. The jarring impact loosened his grip and sent him plunging headlong to the forest floor.

Tom landed awkwardly, his sword and shield bouncing away into the undergrowth. He heaved his way up through the branches, but winced as he put weight on his right ankle. Fear flooded his veins. *If my ankle's broken, I'm finished!*

He hopped behind another tree then paused, feeling his tender ankle with his fingers. Not broken, but sprained. He lowered his foot. Pain seared through his leg – but he could walk on it.

He glanced quickly around the trunk. Slivka was clambering over the fallen tree, ripping at the branches with claws and fangs and hissing angrily as he searched for Tom.

*I'm not that easy to kill,* Tom thought. Slivka reared up, his tongue ripping down thick branches from all around him. Then he brought his claw slamming onto the jungle floor in frustration and rage.

The ground trembled under Tom. Slivka's anger was almost as powerful as Gogmoth's eruption! He had to get away and recover his weapons before he dared to face the deadly Beast.

Tom saw his sword and shield lying in the undergrowth. He hobbled towards them and picked them up. Moving as rapidly as he could through the trees, he made his way back towards the looming volcano. The roars faded slowly away.

A heavy rain of grey ash was pouring from the overcast sky. Gogmoth had stopped erupting, but rivers of moving lava still glowed brightly in the gloom.

Tom could faintly hear Elenna's voice, calling to Silver, but he couldn't see her as he emerged from the jungle. He was on a high ridge surrounded by lava and blazing trees. He hoped the fire wouldn't reach the village.

*Should I go and help Elenna, or should I face the Beast?*

Suddenly, he saw a glimmer of dusky red, stretching out along the ridge of land before them and heading towards the volcano.

*The Warrior's Road!*

Tom watched as the path snaked its way to the foot of the volcano, then wound up the mountain to end at a small dark gash in the rock.

"It's an entrance," Tom gasped. He heard rustling behind him, and spun around. Slivka came slithering out of the trees. His jaws were wide open and his three eyes brimmed with evil.

*Now I have you!* A hissing voice echoed in Tom's mind. He realised with a shudder that he could sense Slivka's thoughts through the power of the ruby in his belt.

The huge lizard-Beast scuttled forwards then reared up, towering over Tom, screeching in triumph as the long tongue lashed down.

Slivka was right. There was nowhere left to run.

# CHAPTER EIGHT

# TRAPPED BY THE BEAST

Tom lifted his shield, deflecting the blow. The tongue gouged a great chunk out of the ground at his feet.

Towering over Tom, Slivka lunged down, his massive horns gleaming in the red light. Tom dropped flat, his shield over his body as the horns thumped into the ground on either side of him. The three eyes burned

with rage. Hot breath blew over him, fouler than the reek of the volcano.

Tom squirmed from between the horns and ran towards the volcano. The pain in his injured ankle seared through him, but he gritted his teeth and forged on.

He glanced over his shoulder. Slivka had wrested his horns from the ground. The Beast reared up on his huge hind legs, fore-claws raking the air, head thrown back as he roared his fury to the skies.

*I've made him angrier than ever,* thought Tom.

The Beast surged after him. Tom speeded up, desperate to reach the gap in the volcano's side. Thick oozing drops of lava spilled over the narrow slot in the rock. Tom hesitated, watching the burning blobs of molten stone falling across his path.

*I hope Elenna and Silver are out of harm's way.*

He could hear Slivka coming closer. "Now!" he panted, lunging forwards, stooping low with his shield over his head. A blob of lava fell by his foot, hissing and spitting. Another sizzled against the surface of his shield. But he made it through the gash in the volcano's side.

Through the cascading molten rock, he saw the Beast approaching.

*I haven't got long*, he thought.

A short tunnel stretched ahead of him, the smooth, glassy stone walls glowing with the reflected light of the lava. Tom crept along it, shield up, sword ready.

Slivka was almost at the entrance, shrieking with rage.

*He's too big to get through without being burned by the lava*, Tom thought with a rush of hope. But Slivka ignored the molten rock as he lowered his head and pushed into the tunnel. Tom saw huge drops of lava splash off the Beast's scaly hide, sparking and sizzling. Burning scales fell away from his body, but he kept on coming. Not even molten rock could stop Slivka.

*How can I ever defeat a creature that walks through lava?* Tom thought.

He ran for the far end of the tunnel as the tongue whipped out again. It licked towards him at knee level, but Tom just had the strength in his injured ankle to leap over it.

He stumbled into a wide, circular cavern. It was like stepping into a raging furnace and the air was so thick and foul that it clogged his throat. All around him were bands of molten rock that seethed and boiled, giving off a fiendish light. Fear clutched his heart. There was no way out!

He spun on his heel as Slivka came crashing into the cavern, claws skittering on the bare rock. Tom darted to the side, desperate to get past the Beast and run back into the tunnel. But Slivka blocked the tunnel mouth, his huge head swaying to focus on Tom.

*Why did the Warrior's Road lead me here if it's a trap?* Tom thought, his shield raised and his sword gripped tightly in his fist.

A crackling sound filled the cavern. Tom saw that the strips of molten rock were widening, oozing trails of lava that spilled onto the floor.

The Beast slunk forwards and Tom saw his fate reflected in the evil eyes.

"I don't fear you, Slivka!" he shouted. "Do your worst!"

Slivka's tongue darted out from between his ferocious teeth. Tom sprang aside, deflecting the tongue with the flat of his blade. Slivka twisted and leaped, this time with his

head down, his deadly horns aimed
straight at Tom.

He sprang aside, but the edge of
one horn struck him hard in the ribs,
crushing him to the ground, knocking
the breath out of him. His sword was
pinned under him, but he beat at the
horn with his shield until finally he
managed to drag himself free and

stagger to his feet again.

Doing his best to keep his weight off his injured foot, Tom backed away around the chamber. Roaring, Slivka scrambled after him, but Tom stabbed with his sword as he ran, aiming for the Beast's eyes, forcing Slivka to turn his head away. As they fought, the walls of the cavern fell to pieces and lava flowed from the widening cracks.

Slivka's claws swept the air, forcing Tom back. The Beast reared up over him, and Tom realised with a sickening lurch that he was in a corner. There was nowhere to run.

*I have to get out*, Tom thought. *It won't be long before lava floods this place and we're both killed!*

A desperate idea grew in his head.

He came to a halt, his arms dropping, his sword and shield

hanging from his fists. Slivka reared up, his three eyes fixed on Tom.

The Beast let out a screech of triumph, arching his neck, opening his jaws. His tongue coiled, ready to deliver the death-blow.

But at the last possible moment, Tom dived forwards. The tongue lashed over him and struck the rocky wall at the very moment that the rock melted into blazing lava.

Slivka gave a screech of agony as his tongue fused onto the molten rock.

Tom hurled himself headlong under the Beast's belly. Slivka's claws scrabbled at the rocks, his eyes rolled in terror, but he couldn't get free.

Tom jumped to his feet. The whole cavern was falling in on itself. Ash and smoke filled the air.

*I have to get out! Now!*

# CHAPTER NINE

# MOLTEN DEATH

Tom ran for the entrance to the
tunnel as rocks showered down on
every side. He paused and looked
back through the heat haze. Lava
poured from the walls.

He peered at Slivka through the
smoke and steam, his eyes stinging.
The Beast shrieked and twisted as he
tried to free himself from the rock.

Pity stabbed through Tom's heart.

He couldn't leave the Beast to be burned alive by the lava. No creature deserved to die in such a terrible way.

He darted back into danger, jumping the flows of lava and feeling in his satchel for the claw of Targro. There was no time to use the ruby to communicate with the panicking Beast – he had to hope that his actions would make his intentions clear to Slivka.

He dived past Slivka's struggling body and sliced the claw across the tip of the Beast's tongue. Black blood spurted from the wound as the tongue came loose from the rock.

Slivka towered over Tom, growling and grunting in pain, his three eyes glaring down. Tom stared up at him, a pang of fear in his heart.

*Was this a big mistake?*

Then Slivka began to fade away, and as the Beast's shape blurred, Tom saw a single scale slip from his neck and come twirling down. Tom reached out, and when he closed his fingers around it, Slivka was gone.

*It's over! But I'm sure he'll return again if anyone else is ever unlucky enough to have to walk the Warrior's Road.*

There was a roar and the crash of the cavern roof falling in. Tom sprang towards the tunnel entrance, a cascade of lava crashing down at his heels. Glancing back, he saw a fiery wall of molten rock rolling towards him.

Despite the agony in his ankle, Tom raced on, pushing the claw and the scale deep into his satchel. The exit from the volcano was now a single sheet of falling lava. Holding his shield above his head and crouching low, Tom flung himself through it. The heat was unbearable and he could smell his clothes sizzling.

Tom came out into the open, gasping and sweating, the smoke rising from his scorched clothing. But horror made him suddenly cold. The lava had spread over the causeway he had used to get to the mountain.

*There's no way back.*

"Tom! Over here!" He stared through the rising smoke. A little way down the mountain, he saw Elenna and Silver standing on one of the few rocks floating in the lava. Elenna was using a long spear almost like an oar to steer towards higher ground.

Tom eyed the distance between him and them. Uninjured, he might just make the jump, but his wrenched ankle wouldn't support him. He couldn't reach her.

"Where did you get the spear?" Tom called.

"From me!" called another voice. Tom stared to a high strip of land on the edge of the jungle. Jenko was standing there, brandishing another spear above his head.

"Catch!" shouted Jenko, hurling the

spear towards Tom.

Tom snatched the spear out of the air. But how would it help him? The rock he stood on was not afloat.

Then he realised. He moved back, took a deep breath, and ran forwards, planting the butt of the spear on the very edge of solid land and flinging himself through the air.

He sailed over the seething lava and landed on Elenna's floating island, stumbling but safe. Silver barked excitedly. The three companions were together again.

"To me," called Jenko, beckoning. "Quickly, before the spears are eaten away by the lava!'

Together, Tom and Elenna pushed the floating rock towards the high spit of land. But the shafts of their spears were on fire now, and all around them

the lava was rising.

"Get closer together," cried Tom as he
saw their island sinking and the lava
creeping ever higher.

Elenna let out a yell of pain and
dropped her blazing spear. Silver howled
in fear. Their floating island had halted –
and solid land was still too far away!

# CHAPTER TEN

# A NEW FRIEND, A NEW ENEMY

"Jump!" Tom shouted to Elenna, lifting his own smouldering spear out of the lava and pushing it into her hands. "Then throw the spear back for me."

She hesitated, then used the spear to vault to where Jenko was waiting to catch her.

Silver crept close to Tom's legs,

whining as the rock sank and the lava crept closer. Elenna flung the spear back but it fell short and sank, burning up in the lava.

Tom looked at Silver. "Jump," he said, pulling his shield off his shoulder. "I'll follow." Silver seemed to understand and launched himself into the air to land safely on the far side of the lava flow.

Tom backed away then ran for the edge of the rock, flinging his shield across the lava and then leaping after it. The pain flared in his ankle and for a terrible moment he thought he wouldn't make it. But his feet came down on the shield, pushing it onward so that he skimmed the river of molten rock.

The shield struck the ridge of land and he jumped off. He spun around,

holding his sword by the point and
using the hilt to grab the leather
straps on the shield and lift it out of
the lava. It was a little scorched, but
otherwise undamaged.

"We have to get away, before we're
surrounded," warned Jenko.

The three companions chased after
Jenko as he ran through the jungle.
Tom struggled along, wincing at the

pain in his ankle, but determined to keep up with the others. He was relieved when Jenko slowed to a walk.

"We should be safe now," said the boy. He looked at Tom. "I saw the Beast chase you into the mountain. What happened?"

"The Beast yielded to me," Tom said simply. "It won't bother you again."

Elenna frowned. "You've hurt your ankle. Here, let me bind it for you." She kneeled in front of him and drew some scraps of linen from her bag.

Jenko looked solemnly at Tom. "I apologise for how I behaved earlier," he said. "You have saved Coshtin Province from a great danger."

"Thank you," said Tom. "I defeated the Beast today, but it will return one day. I need you to pass a message on to your people. If ever they see a boy or a girl walking through their province in the future, they must offer any help they can."

Jenko nodded. "I'll make sure they never forget." He held his hand out and Tom grasped it.

Elenna stood up. "I've bound your ankle as best I can for the time being," she said.

Tom tried his weight on the injured leg. "It's much better," he said with a smile. "Thanks."

"Will you come back to the village?" asked Jenko. "My people will give you a hero's welcome."

"We don't have the time," said Tom. "We have to find the Warrior's Road again and continue on our Quest."

They said their goodbyes to Jenko and he headed off through the jungle.

"How are we going to find the Road again without the map?" asked Elenna.

"Let's go to higher ground," Tom suggested. They walked through the jungle until they came to a hump of bare rock. They clambered up. The sky was still grey with cloud and ash, and behind them part of the jungle was burning. Gogmoth was still spitting flames.

Tom turned slowly, staring down into the jungle.

"While there's blood in my veins, I vow that I will find the Warrior's Road," he muttered under his breath. A rust-red shimmer caught his attention. "There!" He let out a cry, pointing to where the glimmering road snaked through the jungle, away from the volcano.

A wide smile broke out over Elenna's face, even though she couldn't see the Road. "Let's go!" she said.

Tom bounded down the hillside, with Elenna and Silver close behind.

Occasionally the Road would wink out of view, but never for long, and soon it brought them to the very edge of the jungle.

With Tom in the lead, they walked along the mystical Road until it formed a sudden loop around the trunk of a massive old oak tree.

"What's that carved into the tree?" asked Elenna.

Tom had been too intent on watching the road to notice what she was pointing at. Deep grooves had been cut into the bark, forming an oblong shape.

"It looks like a door," he said. He turned to her. "It must be the next portal!" he exclaimed.

Tom stood in front of the tree, his hand on his sword hilt.

"Are you ready?" he asked Elenna.

"It can't be worse than this place," she replied. She frowned at the carved doorway. "But there's no handle or anything. How do we—"

The door suddenly opened, and

strong hands caught hold of Tom's tunic, heaving him towards the portal.

His eyes made just made out a figure in a hooded cloak as he was dragged helplessly into a deep and dreadful darkness.

Join Tom on the next stage
of the Beast Quest, when he faces

# Linka

## the SKY CONQUEROR!

# Beast Quest ®

**FREE COLLECTOR CARDS INSIDE!**

## Series 13: THE WARRIOR'S ROAD
## COLLECT THEM ALL!

The Warrior's Road is Tom's toughest challenge
yet. Will he succeed where so many have failed?

SKURIK
THE FOREST DEMON

978 1 40832 402 8

TARGRO
THE ARCTIC MENACE

978 1 40832 403 5

SLIVKA
THE COLD-HEARTED CURSE

978 1 40832 404 2

LINKA
THE SKY CONQUEROR

978 1 40832 405 9

VERMOK
THE SPITEFUL SCAVENGER

978 1 40832 406 6

KOBA
GHOUL OF THE SHADOWS

978 1 40832 407 3

# Series 14: THE CURSED DRAGON
## COLLECT THEM ALL!

Tom must face four terrifying Beasts as he searches for the ingredients for a potion to rescue the Cursed Dragon.

978 1 40832 920 7

978 1 40832 921 4

978 1 40832 922 1

978 1 40832 923 8

# Win an exclusive
# Beast Quest T-shirt and goody bag!

Tom has battled many fearsome Beasts and we want to know
which one is your favourite! Send us a drawing or painting of
your favourite Beast and tell us in 30 words why you think
it's the best.

Each month we will select **three** winners to receive
a Beast Quest T-shirt and goody bag!

Send your entry on a postcard to
**BEAST QUEST COMPETITION**
Orchard Books, 338 Euston Road, London NW1 3BH.

Australian readers should email:
childrens.books@hachette.com.au

New Zealand readers should write to:
Beast Quest Competition, PO Box 3255, Shortland St,
Auckland 1140, NZ or email: childrensbooks@hachette.co.nz

**Don't forget to include your name and address.
Only one entry per child.**

**Good luck!**

# Fight the Beasts,
# Fear the Magic

# www.beastquest.co.uk

Have you checked out the Beast Quest website?
It's the place to go for games, downloads, activities,
sneak previews and lots of fun!

You can read all about your favourite beasts,
download free screensavers and desktop wallpapers
for your computer, and even challenge your friends
to a Beast Tournament.

Sign up to the newsletter at www.beastquest.co.uk
to receive exclusive extra content and the
opportunity to enter special members-only
competitions. We'll send you up-to-date info on all
the Beast Quest books, including the next exciting
series which features four brand-new Beasts!